THE BIG SURPRISE

Written by Ski Michaels
Illustrated by Diane Paterson

Troll Associates

Billings County Public School Dist. No. 1
Box 307
Medora, North Dakota 58645

Library of Congress Cataloging in Publication Data

———

  The big surprise.

  Summary: On a very special day, Forgetful Freda,
a mouse, cannot remember why she has tied a string
on her finger.
  [1. Mice—Fiction. 2. Memory—Fiction.
3. Birthdays—Fiction] I. Paterson, Diane,
1946-   ill. II. Title.
PZ7.P3656Bi   1986   [E]   85-14017
ISBN 0-8167-0576-3 (lib. bdg.)
ISBN 0-8167-0577-1 (pbk.)

10   9   8   7   6   5   4   3   2   1

THE BIG SURPRISE

Freda was a friendly mouse. She had many friends.

Freda liked her friends. She
liked Mr. Frog. She liked Mrs.
Chipmunk. Most of all, she
liked Mr. Mole.

Freda's friends liked her very
much, too. Why? She was nice.
She was friendly. And Freda
was funny. Oh, was she funny!

What was funny about Freda?
Freda was a forgetful mouse.
She forgot to do this. She forgot
to do that. Freda was always
forgetting things. That is why
her friends called her Forgetful
Freda.

Sometimes Forgetful Freda
forgot to tie her shoelaces.
Sometimes she even forgot to
put on her shoes! Freda did not
want to forget things. She
wanted to remember things. But
she just could not remember
everything.

Sometimes Freda used something to help her remember. What was that something? It was a string. A string tied to her finger helped her to remember.

One day Freda got up early. She
looked out.

"What a nice day," said Freda.

"What will I do today?"

Freda thought.

"Maybe I'll go to visit Mrs.
Chipmunk. Mrs. Chipmunk is
nice."

The little mouse thought some
more.

"Or I could go to Mr. Frog's
house. I like friendly Mr. Frog."

"Or maybe I'll go see Mr. Mole.
He is lots of fun."
Freda thought and thought.
"I know," she said. "I will go
see all my friends."

"First, I'll get dressed," said
Freda. "Then I will go."
Freda dressed. But she did not
go. Forgetful Freda saw
something on her finger.

"Oh no!" Freda cried. "I see a
string. A string is tied to my
finger. That means there is
something I must remember.
But what?"

Freda looked at her finger. She
looked at the string. She tried to
think. What was there to
remember? What? What?
What?

16

"I cannot remember," cried
Freda. "I forgot what I wanted
to remember. Oh, I am so
forgetful!"

Forgetful Freda went out.
"It is still early in the day," she
said. "I will think and think.
Maybe I will remember what I
forgot."

The little mouse went to Mrs.
Chipmunk's house. Mrs. Chipmunk
was happy to see her friend.
"How are you today, Freda?"
she said.

Freda said, "I am forgetful. See
the string on my finger? I do not
know why it is there. I cannot
remember. Can you help me?"

Mrs. Chipmunk looked at the string. She smiled at Freda. Oh, what a forgetful mouse! "I think you wanted to remember to wear your very best dress today," said Mrs. Chipmunk.

"Did I?" asked Freda. "Maybe that is what I forgot."

"Go home," said Mrs. Chipmunk.
"Put on a nice dress. Change
your socks. Put on nice shoes.
And remember to tie the laces.
Then you will look nice. And
maybe then you will remember
what you have forgotten."

Freda went home. She put on a
nice dress. Out came her little
mouse shoes. She put them on.
Freda remembered to tie her
shoelaces.

"Now I look very nice," said Freda. "But I still can't remember what I forgot."

25

Freda looked at the string on
her finger.
"I want to remember," said
Freda. "But I cannot remember.
Maybe Mr. Frog can help."

Freda went to Mr. Frog's house.
Friendly Mr. Frog was happy to
see Freda.
"My, you look nice," he said.

Mr. Frog looked at Freda.
"I like your nice dress," he said.
"I like your nice shoes. You even
remembered to tie your laces."

"Thank you," said Freda. "But there is something I've forgotten." "What is that?" asked Mr. Frog.

"There is a string on my finger,"
said Freda. "But I do not
remember why I tied it on.
Can you help me?"

Did Mr. Frog know? Could he
help Forgetful Freda?

Mr. Frog looked at his friend.
He looked at the string. Oh,
what a forgetful mouse!

"I think I know what you forgot," said Mr. Frog. "You do?" cried Forgetful Freda. "What is it?"

"You wanted to remember to go
to Mr. Mole's house," he said.
Freda looked at Mr. Frog. She
looked at her finger. Was that
what she forgot?

Freda thought and thought.
"No," she said. "That is not
what I forgot. But maybe Mr.
Mole can help me. I will go to
see him right now."

"Oh no!" cried Mr. Frog. "Do not go to Mr. Mole's now! It is too early."

"Early?" said Freda. "Too early for what?"

"Too early for what you cannot
remember," he said. "Excuse
me, Freda. I have to go now."
And away went Mr. Frog.

"What a day!" said Freda.
"Something funny is going on.
I have a string on my finger.
I cannot remember what I forgot.
And Mr. Frog says it is too early
to go to Mr. Mole's house."

Freda went home. She did not
know what to do. She thought
and thought. But she could not
remember anything.

"It is not early now," said
Freda. "Now I will go to see
Mr. Mole."
And away she went.

The little mouse went to Mr.
Mole's house. Mrs. Chipmunk
was there. Mr. Frog was there.

Freda looked at Mr. Mole.
"Do you see this string on my
finger?" she said. "Do you know
what I forgot?"

"I do," said Mr. Mole.
"So do I," said Mrs. Chipmunk.
"I do, too," said Mr. Frog.

"What?" cried Forgetful Freda.
"You forgot that today is your
birthday!" cried her friends.
"Happy Birthday, Freda!"

"My birthday?" said Freda.
"Today?"
She looked at the string on her
finger. Now she remembered!
"It is," cried Forgetful Freda.
"Today is my birthday!"

"This is a birthday party for you," said Mr. Frog.
"It will be a good party," said Mrs. Chipmunk.
"How old are you?" said Mr. Mole.

"How old am I?" Freda cried.
"How old am I? I do not know.
I forgot!"